All-Star Sports Story
series

PLAYOFF DREAMS

FRED BOWEN

PEACHTREE
ATLANTA

Published by
PEACHTREE PUBLISHERS
1700 Chattahoochee Avenue
Atlanta, Georgia 30318-2112

www.peachtree-online.com

Photos of Wrigley Field and Ernie Banks obtained from the National Baseball Hall of Fame Library, Cooperstown, NY

Cover design by Thomas Gonzalez and Maureen Withee
Book design by Melanie McMahon Ives and Loraine M. Joyner

Printed in the United States of America
10 9 8 7 6 5 4 3 2 1
First Revised Edition

Library of Congress Cataloging-in-Publication Data

Bowen, Fred.
  Playoff dreams / written by Fred Bowen. -- 1st rev. ed.
      p. cm.
  Summary: Brendan, the best player on a losing baseball team, learns a les-
son from a Chicago Cubs all-star about the true value of the game. Includes
facts about pitchers, especially Ernie Banks.
  ISBN 978-1-56145-507-2 / 1-56145-507-5
  [1. Baseball--Fiction. 2. Winning and losing--Fiction. 3. Chicago Cubs (Base-
ball team)--Fiction.] I. Title.
  PZ7.B6724Pl 2009
  [Fic]--dc22
                                        2009016867

To my wife and best friend, Peggy Jackson,
who is always working on a dream.

ONE

Crack! As soon as Cubs center fielder Brendan Fanning heard the bat smack the ball, he was off, chasing a high fly ball soaring toward right center field. Brendan's mind was racing as fast as his feet. *Runner on second, nobody out,* he thought. *The runner will be trying to tag up.*

"I got it. I got it," Brendan called out, keeping his eye on the falling ball. Brendan, a lefty, got under the ball, reached up with his gloved right hand, and snagged it out of the air.

The runner at second tagged up and bolted for third base. But Brendan's throw to Josh Cohen, the Cubs third baseman, was right on target. The ball sailed low and hard, skipping once on the infield dirt toward Josh's glove. The runner slid into third base in a cloud of dust and dirt. Leaning over the bag, the umpire spread his arms wide. "Safe!" he shouted.

"What?" Brendan yelped from the outfield. As the base runner brushed himself off at third base, Brendan saw Josh lean over to pick up the baseball lying in the infield dirt.

Brendan's shoulders slumped and he slammed an angry fist into his glove. *My throw was perfect*, Brendan thought as he trudged back to center field, *and Josh blew it*.

Four hits and three runs later, the Cubs jogged slowly off the field. Brendan glanced back at the scoreboard.

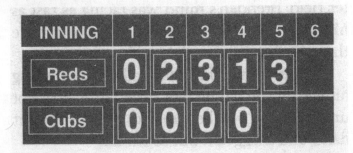

INNING	1	2	3	4	5	6
Reds	0	2	3	1	3	
Cubs	0	0	0			

"Boy, it's gonna be a long season," Brendan muttered to himself.

Mr. DeCastro, the Cubs coach, shouted encouragement to his team. "Come on, kids! Two more innings. We can get 'em back. Top of the order. Michael, Tasha, Brendan. Look those pitches over. We need base runners. Let's get a rally going!"

The inning started badly. Michael Mitchell grounded out to shortstop and Tasha Jackson hit a pop fly that fell right into the center fielder's glove. Brendan stepped to the plate with two outs in the bottom of the fifth inning in a 9–0 game.

Brendan dug his left foot into the back of the left-handed batter's box. He tapped the outside and inside edges of the plate with the end of the bat. Holding the bat loosely in his strong hands, Brendan cocked the bat above his shoulder and stared out at the Reds pitcher. He was ready to hit.

The Reds pitcher fired a fastball toward the inside half of the plate. Brendan uncoiled his strong, smooth swing and lashed the first pitch down the right-field line. He sprinted to first base, thinking about extra bases with every stride. Rounding first base and halfway to second, Brendan looked over his shoulder to see the Reds outfielder still fumbling with the ball. Brendan set his sights on third base and turned on his speed. Fifteen feet from the bag, Brendan hurled himself headlong into third base. Brendan stretched out his hands and grabbed the bag a second before the third baseman slammed his glove into Brendan's back.

Safe! A triple.

Brendan called time out and brushed the dirt from the front of his Cubs uniform.

"Nice hit," congratulated Kyle McCleery, the Cubs third-base coach. "I didn't think you were going to make it."

"No sweat," Brendan replied. "Now let's see if someone can get me home."

But Brendan never got any farther than third base. Cubs pitcher Marcus Cooper sent a high pop fly to the Reds shortstop. Brendan jogged in and touched home plate as the ball settled into the shortstop's glove to end the inning. The score was still 9–0.

Brendan grabbed his glove off the bench and started to run out to center field when Mr. DeCastro stopped him.

"I'm going to give Amy a chance to play center field for an inning, Brendan," the Cubs coach said. "You take the rest of the game off." As Brendan turned toward the bench with his head hanging low, Mr. DeCastro patted him on the back and said, "Nice hit. We're going to need a lot of hits like those from our star player this year."

Brendan took a seat at the end of the bench, stretched out his legs, and watched the rest of the game. He knew it was hopeless. The Reds added two more runs in the top of the sixth while the Cubs went down in order to end the game.

Mr. DeCastro tried to take the sting out of the 11–0 loss. "Tough game, kids. We'll get 'em next time. There are still a lot of games left this season."

Brendan and Josh gathered their equipment from the Cubs bench.

"You heading home?" Josh asked. He and

Brendan lived on the same street.

"Yeah," Brendan nodded. The two friends trudged up a long hill leading away from the baseball field.

"Sorry about that throw in the fifth inning," Josh said, breaking the silence. "It was right in my glove. No way I should have missed it."

'That's okay," Brendan lied and kept walking.

"Man, 11–0!" Brendan finally blurted out as the boys neared their street. "Looks like we're never gonna make the playoffs."

"We can still do it," Josh said bravely. "Remember what Mr. DeCastro said, 'There are still a lot of games left this season.'"

Brendan laughed. "That's what worries me," he said, turning for home.

TWO

Brendan heard the music the moment he stepped inside. The sounds of a piano danced on the warm spring air. Brendan followed the music to the sun-filled back room of the Fannings' large, rambling house.

There, Brendan's father, Tom Fanning, sat at the piano with his back to the door. Next to him, leaning over a big wooden bass fiddle, was the familiar figure of Leon "Skeeter" Wells.

Brendan stood silently in the doorway and listened. His father and Skeeter played together like longtime musical teammates, weaving the sounds of the piano and bass into a mysterious, magical mix. Without thinking, Brendan began to move his foot up and down to the beat.

As the last notes echoed from the bass, Skeeter lifted his eyes up to Brendan as if he were coming out of a trance.

"Hey, little man," he chuckled, his broad face breaking into a smile. "How did the Cubs do today?"

"We lost again, Mr. Wells."

Brendan's father turned on the piano bench and asked, "What was the score?"

"11–0," Brendan muttered, almost embarrassed.

"11–0," Skeeter repeated, waving his hand in front of his nose. "Man, you guys stink as bad as the real Cubs."

Brendan knew Skeeter was joking, but somehow he did not feel like laughing.

"Don't worry," Brendan's dad said. "There are plenty of games left in the season."

Brendan sighed. "That's what the coach said, but I don't think we can win enough of them to make the playoffs."

"Make the playoffs!" Skeeter laughed. "Any team named the Cubs is going to have a tough time making the playoffs. The real Cubs don't usually make the playoffs."

"Boy, I'd like to make it just once," Brendan wished out loud.

"Maybe this will be your year," his dad said softly.

Brendan wanted to change the subject. "You're not a Cubs fan, Mr. Wells. How come?"

Skeeter shook his head. "They're North Side. I'm from the South Side of Chicago. I'm a White Sox fan all the way. I don't go switching around my teams. The 'Pale Hose,' they're my team."

"My Uncle Jack is a big, big Cubs fan," Brendan said.

"Hey, that reminds me," Brendan's dad said. "You should e-mail Uncle Jack and tell him about the game. You promised Mom you would."

"Where is Mom?"

"She's at the hospital delivering a baby. Mrs. Wacker is having her fourth. Now get going, and write Uncle Jack while you're still thinking about it."

"Okay," Brendan said, turning to leave. "See you later, Mr. Wells."

"See you around, little man," Skeeter replied.

Brendan raced up the stairs and into an office cluttered with his mother's medical books and his father's musical instruments. Still in his dirt-stained Cubs uniform, Brendan sat down at the family computer and logged on.

Dear Uncle Jack—

We lost again today. We got creamed 11–0 by the Reds. I got a triple with a headfirst slide and everything, but nobody else did anything. I don't want to brag or anything, but I am the only really good player on the team.

We've played all the teams once and we're tied for last place. Here are the standings:

Reds	5–0
White Sox	3–2

Marlins	3–2
Yankees	2–3
Rockies	1–4
Cubs	1–4

The best four teams make the playoffs for the town championship. I've been playing for four years, and I've never even made the playoffs once! It doesn't look good for this year. Oh well...

Mom and Dad are fine. School kind of stinks. Hope you come for a visit soon.

Your nephew,
Brendo

Brendan looked over the letter and moved the computer cursor to "Send." With a click the letter soared into cyberspace.

Brendan shut down the computer and walked down the hall to his bedroom. Slumped on the edge of his bed he thought, *Man, 11 to zip*! He pulled his Cubs shirt slowly over his head and tossed it on the floor.

THREE

A few days later, Brendan and Josh sat in the sunshine on the steps in front of Josh's house.

"You want to get our gloves and play catch?" Brendan asked Josh.

"Nah," Josh answered, shaking his head. "I'm kind of tired of baseball."

"What? We're not going to get any better if we don't practice," Brendan said, a little too loudly.

"We practice plenty with the team," Josh replied. "Hey, I got it," Josh said, his face brightening. "How about going to the park and tossing the Frisbee around? It's kinda like catching fly balls."

"No, it's not. It's kinda like catching a

Frisbee. We should be practicing catching baseballs," Brendan complained.

"Come on," Josh pleaded. "It'll be fun."

Brendan took a deep breath and gave in. "Oh, all right," he said. "It beats sitting around here."

Before long, the two friends were at the park in the open space behind the baseball field. The Reds were practicing on the baseball diamond. The sights and sounds of the Reds practice made Brendan wish that he were playing baseball. But soon Brendan was running with easy, graceful strides, chasing the Frisbee that sailed and swooped on the cool spring breeze.

"Here's a long one," Josh called, pulling his arm back and letting a high throw go.

Brendan gave full chase, sprinting back toward the fence and reaching out for the flying disk. But the Frisbee tipped off the edge of his fingertips and drifted over the outfield fence and onto the baseball field. Brendan stood at the fence and called out to a Reds player.

"Hey, Ryan. How about a little help?" he

called, pointing to the Frisbee lying on the grass.

Ryan Martinez, star outfielder for the Reds, reached down and flipped the Frisbee over the fence to Brendan.

"Thanks. Hey Ryan, how did you guys make out against the Yankees the other night?"

"We won 7–3."

"Good." Brendan smiled. "That helps us. We gotta beat them to make the playoffs."

"Playoffs?" Ryan laughed. "You guys will never make the playoffs. Especially tossing a Frisbee around."

"We're just fooling around," Brendan said, a little embarrassed.

Just then, a fly ball came soaring out to center field. Ryan moved easily to his left and caught the ball with the cool assurance of an all-star.

"Come on, Brendan!" Josh called from across the field. "Are you still playing?"

Ryan threw the ball back into the infield and then said over his shoulder with a laugh, "Yeah, Brendan, why don't you go

14

back to playing Frisbee? Maybe you guys will make the Frisbee playoffs."

Brendan gripped the Frisbee tightly with his fingers and sent a low hard shot back to Josh.

"Hey, take it easy," Josh called out. "That one almost took my hand off."

Brendan started walking away quickly from the baseball field. "Let's get out of here," he said to Josh. "I'm sick of playing Frisbee,"

As the sun set and a cool breeze kicked up, the two friends headed home. Ryan Martinez's laugh seemed to follow Brendan all the way back to his door.

Brendan's mother was on the phone when he walked into the kitchen. Brendan opened the refrigerator and grabbed a cool drink and plopped down on a chair at the kitchen table.

Brendan's mother hung up the phone and looked at him.

"I'm going to have to go to the hospital tonight. Looks like Ms. Fox-Murphy is going to have her baby," she told him as she checked her watch.

"You mean Amy's mom?"

His mother nodded.

"Why can't she have her baby during the day? Your patients are always having babies at night," Brendan complained.

"I'm sorry, Brendan, I know my schedule has been pretty crazy lately," she said. "But I got Daniel to come over until Dad gets home."

"Daniel! Great," said Brendan. "But where is Dad?"

"He and Mr. Wells are playing a concert at the college. He should be home by 11:00." Brendan's mom started dialing the phone. "Oh," she said, "I almost forgot. Uncle Jack sent you an e-mail today. I printed it out for you and left it on the dining room table."

Brendan ran to the dining room and found the letter. He sat down and read it quickly.

Brendo—

Sorry to hear about your latest loss. Sounds like you Cubs are running into some tough luck—just like the real Cubs. Don't let the losses get you down. You've always got to be thinking: "Let's play two." (I'll explain later.)

Your mom tells me you don't have a game next weekend. I'll be coming for a visit and I've got a surprise that I'm sure will cheer you up. It will be good to see you guys.

Till then, good luck in your next game. Go Cubs!

Uncle Jack

Brendan put the letter on the dining room table and looked out the window. *What kind of surprise is Uncle Jack planning*? he wondered.

FOUR

Let's go, Cubs!" Brendan shouted through the chain-link fence of the Cubs dugout.

He glanced out at the board in center field.

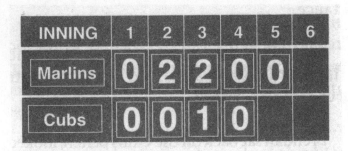

INNING	1	2	3	4	5	6
Marlins	0	2	2	0	0	
Cubs	0	0	1	0		

We'd better rally soon, Brendan thought as he sat on the bench and watched Josh walk up to the plate.

"Come on, Josh, start us off, buddy!" he shouted.

Josh dug in at the plate and stared out at the Marlins pitcher.

A fastball whistled in. Josh never moved the bat off his shoulder.

Strike one!

Josh stepped out of the batter's box and took a deep breath.

"Come on, Josh! Be a hitter. Be a hitter!"

The Marlins hurler wound up and threw another fastball. Again, Josh watched it zip by.

Strike two!

Josh stepped out of the box and took a practice swing. Then he settled into his stance.

"Come on, Josh. Only takes one!"

The Marlins pitcher reached back and fired hard. Josh's bat flashed across the plate but came up empty.

Strike three!

Brendan sat back on the Cubs bench, looked down at the dirt, and kicked away a stone.

"Come on, Amy!" he shouted through cupped hands to the next Cubs batter. "Get us started."

Josh slammed his bat down and slumped beside Brendan on the Cubs bench

"Man, I can't buy a hit," he grumbled, sounding beaten. "I gotta be 0 for my last 10 at bats."

"Don't worry, Brendan said, trying to be helpful. "You'll get another chance. We're gonna start hitting his guy."

Brendan's prediction did not come true. The Cubs could only manage an infield hit squeezed between two more strikeouts. The Cubs took the field in the top of the sixth and final inning still trailing, 4–1.

"Come on, Lucas. We gotta hold 'em," Brendan called from center field. "Throw strikes!"

The Cubs pitcher, Lucas Druskin, was in hot water right away. The leadoff Marlin batter cracked a single right up the middle that Brendan scooped up and hustled back into second base.

Runner on first. No outs.

Josh picked off a hard smash at third for the first out of the inning, but another single put Marlin runners at first and second bases with one out.

Brendan paced nervously around the outfield as the next Marlin hitter took his practice swings and then stepped into the batter's box. *Lucas can't give up any more hits this inning*, Brendan thought, sneaking another peek at the scoreboard. *If the Marlins score again, it will all be over.*

"Bear down, Lucas," Brendan pleaded from center field. "Fire hard! No batter, no batter!"

But the Cubs right-hander was tired, and the next pitch floated over the fat part of the plate.

Smack!

The Marlins batter scorched a sinking line drive to right center field. Brendan sprinted full speed to his left, keeping low to the ground. At the last instant he leaped, straining his arm and stretching his glove out in front of him, desperately trying to catch the fast-flying ball. As he skidded across the outfield grass on his stomach, Brendan felt the ball wedge into the pocket of his glove, just inches above the ground.

Tumbling over, his hat flying, Brendan scrambled to his feet. He checked his glove and found the ball still safely inside. He held the ball up in his left hand to show the umpire.

"Out!" roared the umpire, punching a fist into the air.

Then, quickly eyeing the infield, Brendan threw the ball to the Cubs second sacker, Tasha Jackson. The Marlin runner on second, thinking the sinking liner was a sure hit, had long since rounded third base and was heading for home. He could only watch helplessly, with his hands on his hips, as Tasha joyously stomped on second base for the final out.

Double play!

The Cubs were out of the inning and they still had a chance to win the game!

FIVE

Brendan's catch brought the Cubs bench back to life. Shouts filled the dugout as the Cubs came in for their last at bats.

"All right! DP!"

"Circus catch!"

"Come on, Cubs. It's comeback time!"

Mr. DeCastro called out the batting order above the excitement. "Max, Michael, Tasha. Then Brendan, Marcus, and Josh. Look 'em over. We need base runners."

Max followed Mr. DeCastro's instructions to the letter and worked the Marlins pitcher for a leadoff walk.

Michael Mitchell struck out swinging, but Tasha Jackson brought the Cubs to their feet again by slapping a single to center.

"Way to go, Tasha!"

"Clutch hit!"

The Cubs had runners on first and second, with one out, when Brendan took a deep breath and stepped into the batter's box. The first pitch sailed by high.

Ball one!

Brendan stepped out of the box to study the Marlins pitcher, who was rubbing the baseball and tugging at the bill of his cap.

He's gotta be tired, Brendan thought, *I'm going to try and drive the first good pitch I get*.

The next pitch was right where Brendan liked them, inside corner, belt-high. Brendan swung hard and drilled a screaming line drive to right field.

The Cubs runners were off the moment the ball was hit, racing toward home plate. Brendan whirled around first base and slid into second. Bursting with excitement, he popped up on the bag and yelled, "All right!"

Two runs had scored. The Cubs were only down by one run, 4–3.

As Brendan caught his breath at second

base, Mr. Fields, the Marlins coach, walked slowly out to the mound.

Standing on the mound, Mr. Fields patted his pitcher on the back, took the baseball from his glove and motioned out to the shortstop. The Marlins were bringing in a new pitcher.

Marcus stepped back from home plate and let the new right-hander get in a few warm-up pitches. Standing at second, Brendan studied the new hurler.

Man, this kid throws hard, Brendan thought as the ball smacked up against the catcher's mitt.

"Come on, Marcus," Brendan called from second base. "Bring me home. Just meet it."

Marcus Cooper, the Cubs first baseman, worked the count to three balls, two strikes, but struck out swinging on a blazing fastball. The Cubs were down to their last out.

"Come on, Josh," Brendan pleaded, clapping his hands nervously. "Be a hitter!"

Josh stepped to the plate. The first pitch blazed by the Cubs third baseman before he moved a muscle. Strike one.

Brendan was desperate on second base. *Josh is never going to get a hit off this guy,* he thought. *If I could get to third base, maybe I could score if a pitch gets by the catcher. This pitcher is pretty wild.*

The next pitch came in low and skipped in the dirt off the catcher's shin pads and bounced a few feet away.

Brendan saw his chance and sprinted to third base. The Marlins catcher recovered quickly, grabbed the ball out of the dirt, and pegged a perfect throw to third.

The ball arrived just as Brendan leaped into his slide, stretching his leg for the bag. The Marlins third baseman's glove slammed swift and sure against Brendan's leg.

"Out!" the umpire called. Brendan fell back and lay in the dirt for a long moment, staring at the cloudless evening sky as the Marlins celebrated around him. Slowly, Brendan got up and walked to the silent Cubs bench, dirt and defeat still clinging to his uniform.

Once again, Mr. DeCastro tried to encourage the downhearted Cubs. "Tough loss, guys. We'll get them the next time. You played hard. No game this weekend. We play the Yankees on Tuesday. We'll get back on the winning track with that one."

Brendan gathered his glove and hat from the Cubs bench. As he was leaving, Mr. DeCastro grabbed him by the arm.

"What were you thinking, Brendan?" he asked, but he didn't wait for an answer. "You *never* make the last out of the inning at third base! You're my best player. I need you to play a little smarter than that, okay?"

Brendan nodded and Mr. DeCastro turned to gather up the Cubs equipment. Brendan knew that Mr. DeCastro was right. He shouldn't have made the last out of the inning at third base, but he didn't know what else he was supposed to do. *I can't wait around for someone else to drive me in. I'm the only kid on the team who can really play*, he thought, kicking the dirt as he walked away.

Josh was waiting for Brendan near the outfield fence.

"Are you heading home?" Josh asked.

"Yeah," Brendan answered.

"Did you bring your bike?"

"No, I walked."

"Same here."

The two teammates walked home in silence. Brendan kept thinking about the game. His anger and disappointment seemed to grow with each silent step.

"It was a pretty good game," Josh said finally. "At least it was close."

"We lost, Josh," Brendan said, biting off his words.

"Hey, what did Mr. DeCastro say to you at the end?" Josh asked.

"He said that I shouldn't have made the third out at third base."

"Oh," Josh said. "I guess he's right."

"Yeah, well, maybe I wouldn't have made the last out if you'd get a hit every once in a while," Brendan snapped back.

"What's that supposed to mean?" Josh asked defensively.

"Just what I said."

"Maybe I would get a hit if I got a chance to swing at more than one pitch." Josh's eyes were blazing as he stepped in front of Brendan.

"Fat chance," Brendan said. "You were never going to get a hit off that guy."

"Who says?" Josh shot back. "You're not the only guy who can hit on the team."

"Sure seems like I am," Brendan muttered.

For a long breathless moment, the two boys stood in front of one another. Josh clenched his fists.

Brendan stepped around Josh and walked toward his house. "Why don't you go and find someone to toss the Frisbee with," Brendan called back over his shoulder.

"You think you're such a hero!" Josh shouted. "Why don't you go find another team?"

I wish I could, thought Brendan.

SIX

Brendan did not hear the music as he stormed into the house. He slammed the door and tossed his glove against a chair.

"Is that you, Brendan?" his father called from the back of the house.

"Yeah, it's me," Brendan answered, standing at the bottom of the stairs.

"Is everything okay?"

"Yeah, fine." Brendan started up the stairs.

"Brendan, could you come here? I'd like to talk to you."

Brendan sighed. He did not feel like talking. He walked slowly down the stairs through the living room and into the back room.

Brendan's father sat on the piano bench, his body turned to face the doorway. Skeeter Wells fiddled with the strings of the bass. The long, low notes filled the room.

"Hi, Mr. Wells," Brendan said, stepping into the room.

"Hey, little man, how did the Cubs do tonight?"

"We lost, 4–3."

"Sounds like a tough game," Brendan's dad said. "You okay?"

Brendan looked back into the living room. "Yeah, Dad, I'm okay," he answered, though he knew he did not sound okay.

"You sure?" Brendan's father tilted his head slightly and waited. "You made a lot of noise when you came in."

Skeeter fiddled a few more notes.

"Well...," Brendan started. "I guess...I sort of...you know, messed up and lost the game."

"Did you strike out?" his father asked.

Brendan shook his head. "No, I got thrown out at third base for the last out of the game."

"Oooh," Skeeter groaned, plucking a sad, low note. "You should never make the third out at third base."

"I know, I know," Brendan said. "That's what Coach DeCastro said."

"Is that a rule or something?" Brendan's father asked.

Brendan rolled his eyes and looked away. *How can Dad be so smart and not know anything about baseball?* he thought.

"It's sort of a rule of thumb," Skeeter explained. "The runner doesn't want to take a chance at being thrown out at third because he could probably score from second base just as easily. With two outs, the runner would be running on any ball hit by the next batter."

"But there was no way Josh was going to get a hit," Brendan protested.

"How do you know," his father asked.

"Well, I didn't know for sure. But he hasn't gotten a hit in so long, I figured I had to do something to help win the game."

Skeeter chuckled. "You were at second base," he observed. "Sounds like you had done something already. Did you get a hit?"

"Yeah, a double."

"Any runs batted in?"

"Two."

"Seems like you'd done plenty."

"Yeah, but..." Brendan started.

"I think what Skeeter is telling you," his father interrupted, "is that it is a team game." Skeeter nodded in quiet agreement as Brendan's dad continued. "You can only do the best you can do, then it's up to your teammates. You can't hit for Josh."

"Yeah, but you don't understand, Dad."

"Oh, I think I do, Brendan. I never played team sports, but it seems a little like playing music." Brendan's father turned on the piano bench and started to play a jazzed-up version of "Take Me Out to the Ballgame" on the piano. Skeeter joined in. The two musicians smiled. Brendan's father said over the song, "You see Brendan, I can't play the bass."

"Wouldn't want you to." Skeeter laughed.

"I have to trust Skeeter to do his job."

"I've got you covered, man," Skeeter said, thumping the bass.

"Just the way you have to trust Josh to

do his part. And if Skeeter makes a mistake, I don't yell at him. That's not being a good teammate. Understand?"

"I guess so," Brendan said, without really meaning it. *Dad may know about music and a lot of other stuff*, Brendan thought as he listened to the music, *but this is sports and sports are different.*

After the last few notes faded away, Brendan's father turned on the piano bench and said, "You'd better get out of that dirty uniform. Your Uncle Jack will be here any minute."

"Uncle Jack!" Brendan shouted, remembering the letter.

"And he's got a surprise for you, so hurry up!"

All right, Uncle Jack! Brendan thought as he walked toward the stairs. *Uncle Jack will understand. Uncle Jack knows sports.*

Just then, the front door swung open and Brendan's Uncle Jack popped into the room with a beat-up gym bag on his shoulder and a battered Cubs hat on his head.

"Brendo!" he called out in a booming voice.

"Uncle Jack!" Brendan ran and gave him a bear hug. Their Cubs baseball hats bumped and tumbled to the floor.

"How'd you do tonight?" Uncle Jack asked, pointing to Brendan's uniform.

"Lost again. 4–3."

"Any hits?"

"Yeah, a single and a double. I drove in two!"

"My man!" Uncle Jack shouted as the two exchanged high fives.

"Oh, and I made a great catch," Brendan remembered breathlessly. He demonstrated the catch by diving across the hall rug.

"Well," Uncle Jack said, smiling and reaching into his shirt pocket, "a future major leaguer like you should go and see the real thing."

"What are those?" Brendan asked.

Uncle Jack fanned two tickets in his right hand.

"Tomorrow. Wrigley Field. 3:05. You and I are going to see the real Cubs play the Reds."

Brendan stared at the tickets. His eyes were as wide as dinner plates.

"All right!" he exclaimed. "I haven't been to Wrigley Field since I was about five years old."

Uncle Jack's head snapped back in surprise. "You're kidding," he said. "Looks like I got here just in time."

Brendan held the tickets. *Yes*, he thought, *Uncle Jack got here just in time.*

SEVEN

The next morning, Brendan and Uncle Jack talked nothing but baseball over breakfast.

"I want to get there early," Uncle Jack said. "Grab some lunch, maybe watch batting practice. And don't forget to bring your glove. You might catch a fly ball where we're sitting."

"Where are our seats?" Brendan asked.

Uncle Jack looked surprised. "The bleachers, of course. We're bleacher bums."

Chicago was pretty far away, but somehow the ride did not seem long. Brendan and Uncle Jack talked sports and Uncle Jack played old rock-and-roll tapes, singing along and tapping out the beat on the steering wheel of his clunky old convertible. Uncle

Jack also talked about memories of the Cubs from when he was a kid.

"I remember the first time I went to Wrigley Field," Uncle Jack said as the car sped through the flat Midwestern countryside. "Saw the Cubs play the Cardinals. Bob Gibson pitched for the Cardinals. Man, the Cubbies couldn't touch him. I sat next to my dad—your grandfather—with my glove and a Cubs pennant, waiting for something to cheer about."

Uncle Jack laughed at the memory. "Never came. Cubs must have lost something like 8–0. They couldn't have had more than three hits."

"You've seen the Cubs win, haven't you, Uncle Jack?" Brendan asked.

"Sure. Saw them win a bunch of games in 1969. Cubs almost won the pennant that year. I was at Wrigley Field when Ernie Banks hit his 500th home run."

"When was that?"

"May 12, 1970," Uncle Jack said, as if he were reciting an important date in world history. "He hit it off of Pat Jarvis of the Atlanta Braves."

"I don't remember the last time I was at Wrigley Field," Brendan said as he watched the countryside rush by. "I was too little."

"Good." Uncle Jack smiled. "Then this will be like your first time."

A few more songs and memories later, Jack's car was crawling through city traffic on Addison Street. Finally, Uncle Jack turned into the parking lot near the park.

'There it is," Uncle Jack said, pointing to the front brick wall of the ballpark. He stepped out of his car and shut the door.

Brendan caught his breath as he gazed past the bustling crowds to the ballpark that rose like a great cathedral from the city streets.

"Let's go grab some lunch," Uncle Jack suggested.

"Are we going to eat over there?" Brendan asked, pointing to a fast-food restaurant.

"No way!" Uncle Jack said. "Let's go to Yak-Zies on Clark Street."

As Brendan and Uncle Jack made their way through the crowds near the park, the air was filled with the sounds of a baseball afternoon.

"Programs, programs, get your programs right here!"

"Cubs hats, twenty dollars!"

"Pea-nuts! Pea-nuts!"

Brendan and Jack sat down at a table at Yak-Zies facing an open window, looking out on the bright sunshine on Clark Street.

"What do you two guys want today?" the waitress asked.

"We want the Cubs to win one," Uncle Jack said with a smile.

'Sorry. That's not on the menu," the waitress replied wearily.

"What's good?" Uncle Jack asked.

The waitress tapped the menu with her pencil. "People like the burgers. I like the grilled chicken special."

"I'll have a burger, fries, and a Coke," Brendan answered quickly.

Uncle Jack eyed Brendan then said, "So the future major leaguer's going for a burger? I'll have the chicken special."

After lunch, Brendan and Uncle Jack walked down Waveland Avenue. The block in back of Wrigley Field was closed to traffic. Along the street, kids and grown-ups roamed freely, some wearing baseball gloves and some staring up at the blue skies above the field.

"What are all these people doing out here with gloves?" Brendan asked.

Uncle Jack pointed to the wall along Waveland. "That's the left-field bleachers wall. They're hoping someone hits one out during batting practice."

Uncle Jack looked up. "Here comes one!" he shouted.

Brendan turned and saw a baseball rocket over the wall, bounce high off the pavement of Waveland Avenue, and hit against the low brick houses across the street. Suddenly, the street was alive with people scrambling for the ball. A boy about Brendan's size finally gathered it in. He proudly held it high as he ran down the avenue.

Uncle Jack smiled and then nudged Brendan. "Come on, we go in Gate N, across from Murphy's Bleacher Bar."

The street grew more crowded at the corner of Waveland and Sheffield, near Gate N. Brendan and Uncle Jack shortened their steps. He poked Brendan from behind and pointed to the buildings on Sheffield. "Take a look at the people on top of the houses across the street."

On top of the three-story buildings down Sheffield Street sat rows of metal grandstands. Brightly colored awnings protected the fans from the hot sun. Huge Cubs flags flapped in the breeze.

"Can they see the game from up there?" Brendan asked.

"Sure!" Uncle Jack answered. "People watch the games from up there all the time. Here's your ticket."

Brendan handed over his ticket and walked into the cool dark under the Wrigley Field bleachers. The air smelled of spilled beer and grilled hot dogs. The sounds of baseball echoed inside.

"Ballpark dogs, get your ballpark dogs!"

"Beer here. Get your cold beer."

"Programs! Five dollars. Get your programs right here."

Brendan and Jack walked through a narrow tunnel past a man with a T-shirt that read "I'd Rather be at Wrigley Field," and stepped into the brilliant sunshine. Brendan's eyes took a moment to adjust. Then he took it all in.

Wrigley Field. The smooth green grass of the outfield. The geometry of the infield with four white bases set like jewels in the brown infield dirt. The red brick of the stadium wall. The dark green of the stands. The dappled colors of the Wrigley Field fans.

Uncle Jack put his hand on Brendan's shoulder. "Welcome to the friendly confines of Wrigley Field," he said.

Brendan stood stone-still, gazing about in silence.

"Feel the breeze." Uncle Jack lifted his Cubs hat and ran his hand through his hair. "It's blowing out. Look at the flags in left field."

Brendan looked. "Why does the top flag have a number 14 on it?"

'That was Ernie Banks's number," Uncle Jack explained. "The other flags are for Billy Williams, Ron Santo, and Ryne Sandberg. They were terrific players."

"Was Banks good?" Brendan asked.

"I call 512 career home runs pretty darn good. Let's go find our seats."

Brendan and his uncle settled into their seats just a few rows in back of the ivy-covered red brick wall in left center field. Uncle Jack elbowed Brendan. "Get that glove ready, Brendan. You may see some action."

Just as Uncle Jack predicted, the Cubs and Reds locked into an action-packed slugfest. The Cubs jumped off to an early lead but the Reds came back with a four-run sixth inning, knocking doubles all over the ballpark. The Cubs grabbed back the lead on a three-run homer that sailed over Brendan's head and out of the park. The score was 7–5.

Uncle Jack was on his feet cheering.

"That will make the kids out on Waveland Avenue happy!" he shouted.

But the Reds came back again. In the top of the ninth inning, the Reds put two runners on base with their best slugger coming to the plate.

Uncle Jack fidgeted in his seat. "Come on Cubs! Gotta hold 'em!" he pleaded.

The Cubs pitcher wound up and fired a fastball. The Reds batter connected. The crack of the bat sounded like a pistol shot.

Brendan's outfielder eyes knew the ball was heading for his section the moment it left the bat. Without thinking, Brendan jumped up on his seat and reached his glove above the forest of hands straining for the ball. The ball rocketed straight into Brendan's glove, almost knocking him into the row of seats in back of him.

"I got it!" he shouted to Uncle Jack, holding the ball tight in his glove.

"What a catch!" Uncle Jack yelled. "This boy's going to be a Hall of Famer!"

Brendan could not stop smiling as he stared at the ball safe in his mitt.

"Now, throw it back, Brendo," Uncle Jack called above the buzz of the crowd.

"What?" Brendan asked in disbelief.

"You have to throw it back onto the field," Uncle Jack explained. "Cubs fans never keep a home run from the other team."

Just then, Brendan became aware of the voices around him.

"Throw it back, kid."

"We don't want their homers."

"Come on kid, get rid of it."

For a moment, Brendan stood as if frozen, clinging to his prized baseball. Suddenly, Uncle Jack grabbed the ball from his startled hand. With the crowd cheering, Brendan watched helplessly as the white ball floated out onto the emerald green grass of Wrigley Field.

The ball was gone.

EIGHT

Everything seemed quieter after Uncle Jack threw back the home-run ball.

The Cubs went down without a whisper in the bottom of the ninth inning. Three up. Three down. The disappointed Cubs fans filed silently out of Wrigley Field.

Brendan and Uncle Jack had a quiet dinner at Yak-Zies. The same waitress served them.

"How did they do today?" she asked.

"Lost," Uncle Jack said. He pointed to Brendan. "But the all-star here caught the Reds' game-winning home run."

The waitress looked at Brendan. "Did you throw it back?" she asked.

Brendan nodded.

"Good," she said. "We don't want their home runs. Now, what can I get you guys?"

After dinner, Uncle Jack and Brendan walked back to the car. Jack pointed to the ballpark.

"Look above the center-field bleachers," he said.

There, a blue flag with a white *L* fluttered in the evening breeze.

"What's that?" Brendan asked.

"They fly a flag above the stadium after every game to tell people how the Cubs did. A white flag with a blue *W* means the Cubs won. A blue flag with a white *L* means they lost."

Uncle Jack's car slipped into traffic on Addison Street. "Seems like all I ever see are blue flags," Uncle Jack said, shaking his head.

The noise and lights of the city gradually gave way to the quiet and dark of the nighttime highway. Uncle Jack played softer music on the ride home. It was the kind of music Brendan could imagine his father playing on his piano.

"You okay?" Uncle Jack asked suddenly.

"Yeah, sure," Brendan answered. "Why do you ask?"

"I don't know. You've been kind of quiet. I thought you might still be mad about the baseball. I should have told you before the game about the Cubs tradition of throwing the other team's home runs back."

"That's okay," Brendan lied. "I was just thinking about some other stuff."

"Want to let your Uncle Jack in on it?"

"I was just wondering...I mean...why are you a Cubs fan? They never win anything."

Uncle Jack smiled a tired smile. "I know. The last time the Cubs won the World Series was in 1908. The last time they won the pennant was in 1945."

Uncle Jack paused. He seemed to be silently adding up all those years of lost baseball games.

"But you know," he continued, "the Cubs are my team. I grew up with them. They were my dad's—your granddad's—team. I wouldn't want to root for any other team."

Uncle Jack thought some more and then

kept talking. "It's like your team, Brendo. They aren't winning, but you wouldn't want to play for another team, would you?"

"I don't know," Brendan said. "Sometimes I wish I could play for another team. One that would make the playoffs. I'm one of the best players in the league, and I've never made the playoffs."

Uncle Jack laughed. "Do you remember Ernie Banks?" he asked.

"You mean the guy whose number is on the flag at Wrigley?"

"Yeah," Jack nodded. "Number 14. He played nineteen years for the Cubs and never played in a World Series or playoff game."

"Yeah, but...," Brendan started.

"Yeah, but nothing," Jack said flatly. "Ernie Banks played over 2500 games, hit over 500 home runs and was voted Most Valuable Player in the National League twice. And he usually played for a team that finished near the bottom of the league."

"Man, he must have hated playing for the Cubs," Brendan said.

"Mr. Cub?" Jack asked, almost shocked. "He didn't seem to. You know what Ernie Banks used to say all the time?"

"No."

"He used to say, 'It's a beautiful day for baseball—let's play two.'"

"You put that in your e-mail," Brendan recalled.

"That's right."

"But I don't get it, Uncle Jack. What does it mean?"

"Well, 'let's play two' means let's play two games. I guess Ernie Banks was saying that even though he was playing for a losing team, he was lucky to be playing baseball and he wanted to play baseball all day long."

A truck roared by. After its lights and sounds had faded from view, the road seemed quieter than before. The night was growing cooler. Brendan almost wished that Jack had put the top of the convertible up.

"You know, Brendan," Uncle Jack said, "maybe you should take more of a 'let's play two' attitude about your Cubs."

"What do you mean?" Brendan asked.

"Well, I was just thinking that you're twelve years old, you're playing on a baseball team...you're a pretty lucky guy."

Brendan thought for a moment, "Maybe," he said. "But it isn't much fun when I keep getting hits and making great catches but the team loses because everyone else keeps messing up."

Uncle Jack looked out at the highway. "All you can do is the best you can do," he said. "You can't play the game for everybody else."

"That's what Dad said," Brendan said.

Uncle Jack laughed. "You know, your dad is a pretty smart guy, even if he isn't a baseball fan.

"All I'm saying," Uncle Jack continued, "is that you'd better like playing more than you like winning, because you're going to be doing a lot more playing than winning."

Uncle Jack patted Brendan's shoulder. "Why don't you get some rest," he suggested. "It's been a long day and we've still got a ways to go."

Brendan took his baseball glove and placed it against the corner of the car seat and the edge of the car door. He rested his head against the glove and stared out into the night sky.

He was thinking. He was thinking about the Cubs, the playoffs, Wrigley Field, Ernie Banks, and 'let's play two.' But most of all, he was thinking about the home-run ball that got away.

NINE

Brendan arrived early for his team's game against the Yankees. He leaned against the dugout fence and smiled. The field was quiet. The smell of freshly mowed grass filled the air. The warmth of the day was just beginning to fade.

What a great night for a baseball game, Brendan thought. *"Let's play two."*

Josh Cohen arrived next. Without a word, he walked past Brendan into the dugout.

"You want to warm up?" Brendan asked as he flipped a baseball into the air.

"Okay."

The two boys tossed the ball back and forth in silence.

"I'm sorry about the other day," Brendan said between throws. "I guess I was just sick of losing."

"That's okay," Josh replied. "I just didn't want you to think you're the only kid on the team trying to win."

"Let's go out and have some fun tonight," Brendan suggested.

"Let's win one," Josh said.

"That would sure be fun."

Josh laughed. "It sure would be different."

"Hey, maybe you'll get a hit tonight," Brendan said, smiling.

"Yeah, I hope so."

After all the Cubs had arrived and warmed up, Mr. DeCastro called the team together.

"Come on, kids, big game!" the coach said, clapping his hands together. "We're going to have to beat the Yankees if we want a chance at the playoffs. We're up first, so let's get off to a quick start."

Brendan glanced at the starting lineup on the scorecard that Mr. DeCastro had left on the Cubs bench.

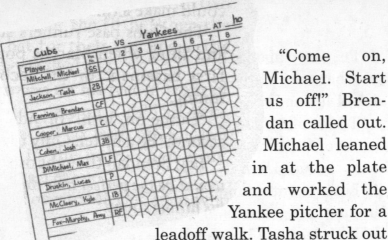

"Come on, Michael. Start us off!" Brendan called out. Michael leaned in at the plate and worked the Yankee pitcher for a leadoff walk. Tasha struck out swinging. Brendan came to the plate tugging at his batting helmet. *One out, runner on first,* he thought. *Make him throw strikes.*

The first pitch sailed by high. Brendan stepped forward but held up his swing. Ball one.

Brendan swung at the second pitch and drilled a line drive to center field. Hurrying to get the ball back into the infield, the Yankee center fielder bobbled the ball. Michael dashed to third base and Brendan made it to second before the Yankee center fielder could make a throw.

The Cubs base runners stayed at second and third when Marcus popped up to the first baseman for the second out of the inning.

56

"Come on, Josh!" Brendan shouted from second. "Be a hitter. Only takes one."

Boy, Brendan thought on second base, *now would be the perfect time for Josh to snap out of his hitting slump.*

The thought was hardly out of Brendan's head when the Cubs third baseman spanked a clean single to left field. The Cubs base runners streaked home. Brendan crossed the plate standing up.

The Cubs led 2–0.

"All right, Josh! Clutch hit!"

"Way to go, Josh!"

The Cubs and the Yankees settled into a seesaw battle. A couple of Cubs errors in the bottom of the second inning allowed the Yankees to knot up the score at 2–2. Brendan smacked a double in the top of the third and scored when Marcus Cooper hit a one-hopper between the Yankee shortstop and third baseman. The Cubs led, 3–2.

But the Yankees came back again with two runs in the bottom of the fifth. When the Cubs came to bat for their last ups in the sixth inning, they trailed 4–3.

Mr. DeCastro was on his feet in front of

the Cubs bench. "Come on, kids! Last licks. We gotta come back. Max leads off, Lucas is on deck, Kyle's in the hole. Then Amy, Michael, and Tasha. Let's go."

Brendan rushed over to Mr. DeCastro, who was holding a clipboard with the Cubs official scorecard.

"When am I up this inning, Mr. D.?" asked Brendan, as he tried to catch his breath.

Mr. DeCastro looked down at the scorecard.

"Seventh," he said, and then looked back to the baseball diamond.

Seventh! Brendan thought. He strained his neck to look at the scorecard to see if it was true.

"Don't worry, Brendan," Mr. DeCastro said. "We're going to get some hits. You'll get up. Just be ready."

Brendan wasn't so sure.

"Seventh," he mumbled to himself.

Brendan pressed his face against the metal link of the dugout fence. *The most important inning of the Cubs season*, he thought, *and I might not even get a chance to swing the bat.*

TEN

"Come on, Max!" Brendan shouted through cupped hands. "Save my ups."

Max DiMichael, the Cubs left fielder, battled the Yankees pitcher, fouling off the pitches to stay alive. Finally, ball four whistled by high and Max trotted down to first base with a hard-earned walk.

"Good eye, Max."

"That's how to start the inning!"

Lucas went down swinging, but Kyle cracked a single that moved Max to second base.

The Cubs had runners on first and second. One out.

Brendan leaned forward on the edge of the bench next to Josh, his elbows on his knees and his hands knitted together as if in prayer.

"Come on, Amy!" he shouted. "Just hit a single!"

Amy Fox-Murphy, the Cubs right fielder, put one foot into the batter's box and leaned back to look at the Cubs bench.

Just outside the Cubs dugout, Mr. DeCastro touched the brim of his cap, clapped his hands together twice, and called out with a booming voice, "Come on, Amy, show 'em where you live!"

On the bench, Brendan and Josh glanced at each other.

"Mr. D. is telling Amy to bunt," Josh whispered.

"I hope he knows what he's doing," Brendan answered.

As the Yankee pitcher went into his windup, Amy squared her feet in the batter's box and held the bat out straight across the front of the plate. The ball plunked against the bat and dribbled down the third base line. The two Cubs runners sprang into action, dashing to second and third. The Yankee third baseman pounced on the ball and threw to first base to get the sprinting Amy by a step.

The Cubs had runners on second and third, two outs.

The Cubs bench was on its feet. Mr. DeCastro shouted above the noise. "Good job, Amy. Michael, you're up. Tasha on deck. Brendan, you're in the hole." He held up two fingers. "Two outs," he reminded the base runners. "You're running on anything!"

Brendan put on a batting helmet as he called out, "Come on, Michael! Save my ups. Be a hitter!"

Michael Mitchell, the Cubs shortstop, stood in at the plate and locked his eyes on the Yankee pitcher.

The first pitch came in low. Michael held back. Ball one. The next pitch flew in a bit higher and Michael slashed a hard single up the middle, just beyond the reach of the diving Yankee shortstop.

Max and Kyle were off at the crack of the bat, legs churning for home. They both crossed home plate standing up, one right after the other. The Cubs had grabbed the lead back, 5–4.

The Yankees brought in a new pitcher, but Tasha kept the rally going with a bloop single over to right field. Michael dashed to third.

"All right, Tasha!" Brendan yelled from the on-deck circle. "Way to keep it going."

Brendan took a deep breath and stepped to the plate. *Runners on first and third*, he thought. *A hit will break the game wide open.* He cocked the bat behind his left ear, rubbing the handle over and over in his hands.

The first pitch was perfect. Brendan swung hard and met the ball right on the sweet spot of the bat. The ball shot off like a rocket.

Brendan bolted from the batter's box but had barely gone two steps when the Yankee second baseman snared the scorching line drive. Brendan kicked the dirt and circled back, head down, to the Cubs bench to grab his glove for the bottom of the sixth inning.

"Come on, Cubs. Let's hold 'em!" Brendan

shouted as he raced out to center field.

For the first time in a long time, the Cubs fielders were full of chatter.

"One-two-three inning!"

"Good defense!"

"Come on, three up, three down!"

The first Yankee batter lofted a lazy fly ball to center field.

"I got it! I got it!" Brendan called, waving his hands as he drifted under the ball. One out.

The second Yankee batter struck out, but the Yankees' hopes stayed alive when their catcher, Bryan Wacker, laced a line drive against the left field fence. Brendan sprinted over and grabbed the ball as it bounced off the wall. He fired the ball back to the infield. Bryan skidded to a stop at second base with a double.

"Come on, Lucas! One more out. Bear down, buddy," Brendan shouted from center as he pounded his glove.

Lucas Druskin fired a fastball.

Crack!

The ball sailed out to right field. Brendan

sprinted over, hoping to make the play. The ball kept drifting away from him, farther over to right field. Brendan could only watch helplessly as Amy moved back a couple of steps, steadied herself, held up her glove, and squeezed the ball for the last out of the game.

The Cubs had won one!

Brendan and Amy traded high fives and the Cubs ran happily off the field.

'That-a-way, Brendan!" called a pair of familiar voices.

Brendan looked along the fence that ran along the left-field line. His mother and father stood clapping and smiling.

"Hey, you made it!" Brendan said, walking over to the fence.

"I got away from the hospital early." His mother smiled. "So I dragged your father away from his piano."

"I should come more often." Brendan's dad laughed. "That was quite a game."

"You'll have to write Uncle Jack about this one," Brendan's mom reminded him.

"I sure will," Brendan answered. "We

really needed this win if we're going to make the playoffs."

"Who knows," Brendan's dad said, "maybe this will be the start of something big."

ELEVEN

A few weeks later, Brendan sat in front of the family's computer, still in his dirty uniform from the day's game. He studied his words on the screen.

Dear Uncle Jack,

The Cubs won again today! We beat the Rockies 9-2. We scored six runs in the second inning (I drove in two with a single) and coasted.

With one game left in the regular season, the team still has a chance to make the playoffs!

Here are the standings:

Reds	11-3
White Sox	9-5
Marlins	8-6
Yankees	7-8
Cubs	6-8
Rockies	2-13

We have one more game against the Reds. We've got to beat them!! If we do, we finish in fourth place and make the playoffs. (We would make the playoffs instead of the Yankees because we beat the Yankees twice.)

The Reds are the best team in the league but I think we can beat them. We have been playing a lot better since you and I went to Wrigley Field.

I've been playing great. I got two more hits today. That makes 20 for the season. I sure hope the season doesn't end after just one more game.

Mom and Dad say hi.

I say, "Let's play two!"

Love,
Brendo

When Brendan finished reading the letter, he moved the cursor to "Send" and clicked.

Brendan's dad opened the door and poked his head into the room.

"Hey, Brendan, writing Uncle Jack about today's big win?" he asked.

"Yeah. One more to go. If we win that one, the Cubs are in the playoffs."

"When's the last game?"

"Day after tomorrow. But I hope it won't be the last game."

Brendan's father's face twisted into a pained expression.

"Day after tomorrow?" he repeated. "It looks like I'll have to miss it. Skeeter and I have a concert in Chicago that evening."

Brendan couldn't hide his disappointment.

"Oh, Dad," he pleaded. "You gotta come. You're our good-luck charm. We always seem to win when you show up."

Brendan's father smiled. "I wish I could go, Brendan. You're making a real baseball fan out of me. In fact, if you and Uncle Jack go to Wrigley Field again, maybe I'll tag along."

Brendan smiled. "That would be fine with me."

"I might see Jack at the concert in Chicago," Brendan's dad said. "It's a fundraiser and I think some of the old players from the Cubs have been invited."

Brendan laughed. "If the Cubs are there, Uncle Jack will be there."

"Well, at least your mom will be at the game," Brendan's dad noted. "Even if she has to wear her beeper."

Brendan laughed. "Just so it doesn't go off in the middle of the game."

Brendan's dad sat on the edge of a chair and looked at Brendan.

"Seems like you've really turned your season around," he said.

"Yeah. Well, I'm doing like you said. I'm doing my best and not trying to win every game by myself."

"Well, I'm glad you learned something from me this season." Brendan's dad smiled, sitting back in his chair. "I know I learned something from watching you play this season."

"What's that?"

"I learned that playing baseball must be as much fun as playing music."

"I guess as long as you're playing anything," Brendan observed, "it's fun."

Brendan's dad put his hands on his knees and rose up from his chair. "Well, Brendan, I'm sorry I'll miss your last game."

Brendan looked up at his father. "It won't be our last game," he said, his voice filled with determination. "We're going to play two. You can come to the second game, Dad."

TWELVE

Bring it in, Cubs!" Mr. DeCastro shouted. Brendan and the Cubs jogged in from their warm-ups. A circle of fidgety blue hats surrounded the Cubs coach.

"All right, kids," Mr. DeCastro started. "Last game."

Brendan interrupted quickly. "If we win, Mr. D., don't we make the playoffs?" he asked.

"That's right, Brendan." Mr. DeCastro smiled. "I meant our last *regular season* game."

The circle of blue hats buzzed with excitement.

"Okay, listen up!" Mr. DeCastro shouted, holding up his hands. "The Reds are the home team, so we have first ups. Here's the batting order. Michael's leading off. Then Tasha, Brendan, Marcus is batting clean-up, Josh, Kyle, Max, Lucas, and Amy. Let's get off to a good start and play heads-up baseball!"

Brendan sat down on the edge of the Cubs bench, wearing a batting helmet and rubbing a bat with his hands. Josh sat down beside him. The two teammates traded quick hand slaps.

"Let's get it started," Josh said.

Brendan looked out at the Reds pitcher and nodded. "It's prime time," he said. "Playoff time."

Michael bounced out to second to start the inning. But Tasha laid down a perfect bunt and raced to first base. The Cubs had a runner on first, one out. Brendan stepped into the batter box.

"Come on, Brendan!"

"Be a sticker."

The Reds pitcher fired a fastball by Brendan, who stepped forward but kept his bat on his shoulder.

"Strike!" the umpire called. His hand flashed up.

This guy throws hard, Brendan thought as he dug his back foot a bit deeper into the dirt. *Come on, get the bat off your shoulder.*

The next pitch came in belt-high. Brendan flashed his bat across the plate and drilled a ground ball past the diving Reds second baseman. Tasha whirled around second and slid into third base. The Cubs had runners on first and third, one out.

"Way to go, Brendan!"

"Good stick, good stick."

Marcus struck out swinging and Josh got two quick strikes swinging at the hard fastballs.

"Hang in there, Josh," Brendan called from first base. "Only takes one."

Josh fought off the next pitch and blooped a short fly ball to center field. The ball fell between three Reds players. Tasha dashed home and Brendan raced around second base and skidded to a stop at third.

The Cubs led 1–0!

Kyle McCleery grounded out to shortstop

to end the inning. Brendan grabbed his glove and hat and dashed out to center field, yelling, "Come on, Cubs, let's hold the lead."

Brendan looked in from center field and broke into a grin.

A big game for the playoffs, he thought. *Just like I always dreamed.*

Brendan's daydreams were interrupted by the sharp crack of the bat. Lauren West, the Reds speedy leadoff hitter, slashed a line drive right to center field.

Brendan dashed across the outfield as the ball skipped along the outfield grass. He reached out and backhanded the ball, dug his left foot into the turf, and fired a hard throw to second base. Lauren, thinking she had an easy double, sprinted past first base with her eyes down and headed for second.

Brendan's throw beat her to the bag. Michael grabbed the ball on one hop and plopped his glove in front of the base. Lauren slid right into the tag.

"Out!" the umpire called.

The Cubs burst into cheers. Brendan and

Amy slapped their gloves together in the outfield.

"Great throw, Brendan!"

"That's how to put the tag on her, Michael!"

Brendan's play seemed to inspire the underdog Cubs. The teams traded the lead in a tight baseball battle. The Reds scored two runs in the bottom of the second but the Cubs tied it up with a run in the third. The Reds snatched the lead back in the fourth when Ryan Martinez smashed a two-out double to drive in a run.

Brendan glanced at the scoreboard as he ran in to the Cubs bench after a scoreless fifth inning.

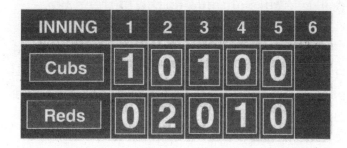

INNING	1	2	3	4	5	6
Cubs	1	0	1	0	0	
Reds	0	2	0	1	0	

Mr. DeCastro was on his feet.

"Last ups, kids. Top of the order. Michael, Tasha, Brendan, Marcus. Eye on the ball. We need some hits."

Brendan paced in front of the Cubs bench, clapping his hands, waiting his turn at bat.

"Rally time! Come on, Michael, get us started!"

Michael brought hope to the Cubs with a single through the Reds infield. The Reds first baseman knocked down Tasha's grounder and scrambled over to first for the out. One out, runner on second.

Brendan took a deep breath before he stepped to the plate. He took a couple of practice cuts outside of the batter's box.

Nice, level swing, he reminded himself.

The Reds pitcher tugged at his cap, went into his windup, and fired. The ball smacked into the catcher's mitt before Brendan could even decide to swing.

Strike one!

The next pitch sailed high and inside. Brendan jumped back.

Ball one.

The Reds pitcher reared and fired again. This time, Brendan was ready. He swung smooth and level, but the ball slanted off the bat and onto the screen in back of home plate.

Foul ball. Strike two.

Brendan's heart raced. *Down to my last strike*, he thought. *Just meet it.*

The next pitch spun in toward the outside edge of the plate. Desperately trying to protect the plate, Brendan lunged at the ball, connecting with the very tip of his bat.

The ball floated out along the right-field line as Brendan dashed to first base.

"Fair ball!" the umpire shouted.

Brendan looked up at first base to see Michael sprinting toward the plate. The Reds left fielder threw the ball home but it was too late! The score was tied 3–3.

Brendan, playing heads-up baseball, scooted to second base and stopped.

"Come on, Marcus!" Brendan shouted breathlessly. "Bring me home!"

But Marcus could not get around on the

Reds pitcher's fastball and struck out swinging. With two outs and the score tied, Josh stepped to the plate.

The Cubs bench was on its feet.

"Come on, Josh."

"Be a hitter."

"Just a bingle, Josh. Just a bingle."

Mr. DeCastro stood on the Cubs bench holding up two fingers. "Two outs, Brendan. Run on anything!"

The first two pitches flew by Josh for strikes. The next pitch skipped in the dirt and fell in front of the Reds catcher. Brendan thought about taking a chance and running for third base but he held back. He remembered Mr. DeCastro's warning, "Never make the third out at third base!"

"Only takes one, Josh!" Brendan shouted.

Josh swung hard on the next pitch and sliced a single to right field. Brendan took off at the crack of the bat. He rounded third base as the Cubs third-base coach, Lucas Druskin, jumped up and down and circled his arms wildly. Brendan streaked across the plate with his arms above his head.

The Cubs had the lead, 4–3.

THIRTEEN

One out later, Brendan grabbed his glove and sprinted out to center field. "One-run lead, Cubs!" he screamed. "Let's play good defense."

Brendan paced the outfield like a caged bear. He looked up at the flag past the center-field fence. The wind was blowing across from right field to left field. He pounded his glove. *Let every ball come to me*, he silently wished.

Brendan got his wish on the first pitch. The Reds leadoff hitter laced a line drive to right center field. Brendan got a good jump on the ball, dashing to his left and stretching out his glove to snag the flying ball.

Brendan tossed the ball back into the

infield. He jogged back into his position holding one finger in the air.

"One out!"

The fielders were full of chatter, encouraging the Cubs pitcher, Lucas Druskin.

"Come on, Lucas, throw hard."

"One-two-three inning, Lucas."

"No batter, no batter."

But Lucas walked the next Reds hitter.

Standing in the outfield, Brendan sensed trouble. He circled the small, brown patch worn in the outfield grass in center field.

"Come on, Lucas, throw strikes!" Brendan yelled at the top of his lungs, "Let 'em hit it!"

Brendan's heart jumped as the next Reds batter belted a towering fly ball to right center field. Brendan raced back toward the fence, his long legs speeding across the green turf. Glancing over his right shoulder and keeping his eye on the ball, Brendan called out, "I got it! I got it!" He slowed his pace to an easy trot, reached out his glove, and snagged the fly ball a few steps in front of the fence.

Brendan rifled the ball back to the infield and the Reds runner returned to first base.

"Nice catch," called Amy.

"Thanks," Brendan said, a bit out of breath. "We were lucky. The wind held the ball up. If he had hit it to left, it would have been long gone."

Brendan walked back to center field.

"Come on, Lucas, one more out!" Brendan shouted, pounding his glove. *Hit it to me, please hit it to me,* he thought as Reds slugger Ryan Martinez stepped to the plate.

Brendan jumped as Ryan swung hard and fouled off the first two pitches. Lucas threw two pitches low and away. Ryan held back. Two balls, two strikes, two outs.

"One more, Lucas. Throw strikes."

Sensing disaster, Brendan was off a split second before the bat hit the ball, sprinting full speed to left center field. He glanced up at the ball riding high in the spring breeze as he hurtled to the outfield fence. *I've got a chance,* he thought frantically.

Brendan could feel the fence coming closer, but he did not slow down. Keeping his eye on the ball, he took a final step and leaped into the air, his glove stretched out, searching for the ball.

Brendan reached over the fence and the ball slammed into the very top of the webbing. *I got it*, Brendan thought, still airborne. But just then his body smashed into the outfield fence. The wooden fence bent under Brendan's weight and then tossed him like a rag doll back onto the outfield grass.

Brendan lay twisted in the grass, a sharp pain shooting up his right side. He lifted his glove and stared into the pocket. It was empty.

Brendan's head fell back onto the grass, a dull ache rising in his right side and the cheers of the Reds team echoing in his ears.

The ball was gone. Long gone.

FOURTEEN

Well, you're lucky. Nothing is broken," the doctor said as she entered the small, brightly lit room. Brendan sat on a couch next to his mother, holding his side. He was still in his uniform.

The doctor sat down in a chair and held up a series of X-rays to the light.

"You just have a bad bruise. But, of course, any bruise around your ribs is going to hurt a while."

"How long will it take to heal?" Brendan's mother asked.

"Oh, I would say a week or so. Let's take another look. Could you stand up again, Brendan?" Brendan stood up. The doctor pulled up his Cubs shirt. Brendan's side was pink and swollen. The doctor shook her head and said, "You must have been running pretty fast. What happened?"

"I was going after a fly ball and crashed into the fence."

"Did you catch it?" the doctor asked.

Brendan looked down at the floor. "No," he said, his voice just above a whisper. "I had it in my glove for a second, but I couldn't hold on to it."

I can't seem to hold on to any home-run balls, he thought.

"Well, it looks as if you gave it a good try," the doctor said.

Brendan tucked in his shirt and sat down again. The pain in his side made him wince. Somehow, right then, trying did not seem to be enough. *If only I had held on,* he thought, *we would have made the playoffs.*

The doctor patted him on the knee. "I'll write out a prescription for medicine that will keep the swelling down. Your mom will take care of you. I know she's a doctor, too."

"She's a baby doctor," Brendan protested.

"You're still my baby," his mother said.

"Mom!" Brendan groaned.

Brendan's mom carefully helped him to the car and drove him home. She propped him up in the big living-room chair and surrounded him with soft, forgiving pillows.

"Let me see if there are any messages," Brendan's mom said as she pushed a button on their telephone answering machine.

After a series of beeps, Brendan heard a familiar voice.

"Hi, this is Mr. DeCastro. It's nine o'clock and I'm calling to see how Brendan is doing. That was almost a fantastic catch. I hope everything is okay."

Brendan smiled as more beeps sounded and another familiar voice came on the line.

"Hello, this is Josh and I wanted to speak to Brendan. I hope he's okay and didn't break anything. I'll call him tomorrow. Bye."

The machine clicked off and Brendan's mother walked back to the living room chair.

"You okay?" she asked.

Brendan nodded silently.

She leaned over and kissed him on the forehead. "See," she whispered, "you are still my baby." This time, Brendan was too tired to disagree.

"I'd better run out to get your medicine," she said. "I'll be back in about ten minutes. Will you be okay? I'll be really quick."

Brendan nodded and settled back into the pillows. "Mom, if I fall asleep, will you tell Dad to wake me up when he gets home? I want to talk to him about the game."

"Sure, but try to get some rest," she said. Then Brendan heard the squeak of his mother's shoes across the floor and the door closing behind her.

The house was quiet. Brendan sat and wished that his father was home already so that he could fill the emptiness with his music. But the music room was dark, the piano silent and still.

Alone in the noiseless night, Brendan let his thoughts wander back to the last play of the game. In the dim light, he could almost see the baseball falling past the outfield fence. He could feel his body rising into the air and his glove, for just the briefest instant, holding on to the baseball. And as Brendan slipped off into a dreamless sleep, he was still holding on.

FIFTEEN

Brendan." Brendan's eyes flickered at the sound. The dim yellow light from a single lamp in the music room cut into the darkness of the living room.

"Brendan."

Brendan turned his head to the gentle voice. Through his sleepy eyes, he could see his father dressed in a black tuxedo, standing above him. Brendan straightened his body in the chair. His eyes narrowed as he felt the pain in his side.

"You okay?" his father asked.

"My side is a little sore."

"Mom told me you guys lost a tough one tonight."

"Yeah, 5-4."

"She said you almost made an unbeliev-able catch to save the game."

The memory of the last play came back to Brendan like the pain in his side.

"Almost," he said. "I had the ball for a second but I crashed into the fence and I couldn't hold on."

"Sounds like you gave it everything you had," his father observed.

"Yeah," Brendan agreed with a tired smile. "But we still lost."

"I'm not so sure," his father replied.

"What do you mean?" Brendan asked. "Sure seems like we lost. The season's over and we're not going to the playoffs."

Brendan's father sat back in the sofa. "You did the best you could. That's all you can do," he said. "Any time you do your best, you never really lose."

"But Dad, they don't let the best player on a losing team into the playoffs," Brendan said, sinking back into the pillows. "They just let the best teams into the playoffs."

Brendan's father raised his head up quickly. "Oh, that reminds me," he said. "I have something for you."

He got up, walked across the living room, and turned on a lamp. Brendan squinted into the light. He saw his father reach into a small bag.

Brendan pushed himself higher in his chair. His father sat down on the sofa again.

"I saw Uncle Jack at the fundraiser tonight. He gave this to me. He said to be sure to give it to you, win or lose."

Brendan's father held out a new, white baseball. Some writing was scrawled across the ball.

Brendan turned the ball in his hands so he could read the writing. It read:

Let s play two,
Ernie Banks

"Uncle Jack said maybe this one could take the place of the baseball you lost at Wrigley Field."

Brendan stared at the words on the baseball.

"You mean Ernie Banks was there?" Brendan asked, his voice rising with excitement. "Dad, he's a Hall of Famer!"

"Yeah." Brendan's father nodded. "Uncle Jack talked to him."

"Wow," Brendan said, and he looked down at the ball to make sure it really was his.

"May I see it?" Brendan's father asked, holding out his hand.

Brendan gave his father the baseball without a word.

His dad looked at the writing on the baseball. "What does 'let's play two' mean?" he asked as he handed the ball back to Brendan.

Brendan thought for a moment. He thought about the Cubs season, how the team had started so poorly but had struggled back. He thought about his talks with his father and Uncle Jack. Finally, he thought about his last desperate grasp at glory. And how his playoff dreams, despite all his efforts, had stayed just past his reach.

"It's kind of hard to explain, Dad," he said. "But it means that even if you lose a game, at least you got to play baseball, and playing baseball is great. And I guess it is like you said. If you do your best, you never really lose."

Brendan's father nodded and patted his son on the knee. "Jack said you would understand," he said as he stood up and motioned toward the stairs.

"Come on, we'd better get you in bed," he said. "And you'd better put that ball in a safe place."

"Don't worry, Dad," Brendan said, smiling from ear to ear. "I am definitely going to hold on to this ball."

THE END

ERNIE BANKS
THE REAL STORY

During his nineteen-year Hall-of-Fame career with the Chicago Cubs, Ernie Banks set at least one record that he wished he had never set. Ernie Banks played in more games than any other major leaguer without ever playing in a playoff game or World Series!

Banks was not the only player whose playoff dreams never came true. Other players who played in a lot of games never saw any post-season glory. And they were good

players too. (You have to be good to play in more than 2,000 big-league games.) Here's a list of some of the most frustrated players in baseball history.

Terrific Players Who Never Made the Playoffs or the World Series and the Number of Games they Played

Ernie Banks, 1953–71	2,528
Luke Appling, 1930–50	2,422
Mickey Vernon, 1939–60	2,409
Buddy Bell, 1972–89	2,405
Ron Santo, 1960–74	2,243
Joe Torre, 1960–77	2,209
Toby Harrah, 1969–86	2,155
Harry Heilmann, 1914–32	2,146
Eddie Yost, 1944–62	2,109
Roy McMillan, 1951–66	2,093

Some pretty good pitchers also never had the chance to pitch in the post-season. Here is a list of some of the "winningest" pitchers (and their career wins) who never pitched in the playoffs or World Series:

Terrific Pitchers Who Never Made
the Playoffs or the World Series
and Their Career Wins

Ferguson Jenkins, 1965–83	284
Ted Lyons, 1923–46	260
Jim Bunning, 1955–71	224
Mel Harder, 1928–47	223
George "Hooks" Dauss, 1912–26	222
Wilbur Cooper, 1912–26	216
Larry Jackson, 1955–68	194
Emil "Dutch" Leonard, 1933–53	190
Mark Langston, 1984–1996	172
"Spittin' Bill" Doak, 1912–29	170

Even among these outstanding players, Ernie Banks stands out. Born in 1931 into a family of twelve children, Banks went on to star in football, basketball, track, and baseball at Booker T. Washington High School in Dallas, Texas. After high school, Banks played professional baseball for the Kansas City Monarchs of the Negro American League, a league made up of black baseball players. In those days America was segregated; black players were not allowed in the major leagues until 1947, and very few blacks played in the majors until the 1950s.

At the end of the 1953 season, Banks and second baseman Gene Baker became the first blacks to play for the Chicago Cubs. Banks, who later was known as "Mr. Cub," was one of baseball's biggest stars. Between 1955 and 1960, he slammed more home runs (248) than any other player. That was more home runs than such big-time sluggers as Henry Aaron, Mickey Mantle, Willie Mays, or Ted Williams. Banks was also named the Most Valuable Player in the National League in 1958 and 1959.

Banks hit a total of 512 home runs. More than half of his homers came in the "friendly confines of Wrigley Field" where the Cubs fans were sure to hold on to any ball belted by Banks. It is true that, at Wrigley Field, Cubs fans throw back home-run balls hit by players on the other team, but they hang on tight to balls blasted into the stands by Cubs players!

Despite Bank's heroics, the Cubs could not get into the playoffs or World Series. But all the Cubs' defeats could not defeat Ernie Banks. Banks was known for his cheery disposition as well as his sure fielding and flashing bat. Banks kept smiling when other players might have given up or asked to be traded. "I never liked losing, but I could take it," he once said. "I loved the game. People want to change it...but I wouldn't change a thing. It's a great game."

Maybe his love for the game of baseball explains why during the ups and downs of his career, Ernie Banks could always say, "It's a beautiful day for baseball—let's play two."

ACKNOWLEDGMENTS

As always, the author would like to thank Scot Mondore at the National Baseball Hall of Fame Library in Cooperstown, New York. This time, Mr. Mondore dug up interesting facts about Ernie Banks.

The author would also like to thank Rick and Scott Hinden for showing him around Wrigley Field.

ABOUT THE AUTHOR

One of Fred Bowen's ear-
liest memories is watching
the 1957 World Series with
his brothers and father on
the family's black-and-white
television in Marblehead,
Massachusetts. Mr. Bowen
was four years old.

When he was six years
old, he was a batboy for his
older brother Rich's Little
League team. At age nine, he played on a team himself,
spending a great deal of time keeping the bench warm.
By age eleven, he was a Little League All Star.

Over a period of thirteen years, Mr. Bowen coached
thirty-one different kids' sports teams in soccer, baseball, softball, and basketball.

He attended his only game at Wrigley Field on a
beautiful afternoon in June 1996. The Cubs lost.

Mr. Bowen is the author of a number of sports nov-
els for young readers. He lives in Silver Spring, Mary-
land, with his wife Peggy Jackson. His daughter is a
college student and his son is a college baseball coach.

Mr. Bowen writes a weekly sports column for kids
in the *Washington Post*.

Visit his website at *www.fredbowen.com*.

Want more?

All-St★r Sports Story Series

Full Court Fever
PB: $5.95 / 978-1-56145-508-9 / 1-56145-508-3

The Falcons have the skill but not the height to win their games. Will the full-court zone press be the solution to their problem?

Off the Rim
PB: $5.95 / 978-1-56145-509-6 / 1-56145-509-1

Hoping to be more than a benchwarmer, Chris learns that defense is just as important as offense.

The Final Cut
PB: $5.95 / 978-1-56145-510-2 / 1-56145-510-5

Four friends realize that they may not all make the team and that the tryouts are a test—not only of their athletic skills, but of their friendship as well.

On the Line
PB: $5.95 / 978-1-56145-511-9 / 1-56145-511-3

Marcus is the highest scorer and the best rebounder, but he's not so great at free throws—until the school custodian helps him overcome his fear of failure.

All-Star Sports Story series